Brooklyn Dodger Days

Written and illustrated by Richard Rosenblum

The Golden Age of Aviation
My Block
Brooklyn Dodger Days

Brooklyn Dodger Days

Written and illustrated by Richard Rosenblum

Atheneum 1991 New York

Collier Macmillan Canada
Toronto
Maxwell Macmillan International Publishing Group
New York   Oxford   Singapore   Sydney

Atheneum
Macmillan Publishing Company
866 Third Avenue, New York, NY 10022

Collier Macmillan Canada, Inc.
1200 Eglinton Avenue East
Suite 200
Don Mills, Ontario M3C 3N1
First Edition
Printed in Singapore
10 9 8 7 6 5 4 3 2 1

Library of Congress Cataloging-in-Publication Data
Rosenblum, Richard.
Brooklyn Dodger days / written and illustrated by
Richard Rosenblum.—1st ed.
p.   cm.
Summary: Re-creates a Brooklyn Dodgers baseball game played
against their rivals the New York Giants in 1946.
ISBN 0–689–31512–0
1. Brooklyn Dodgers (Baseball team)—History—Juvenile literature.
[1. Brooklyn Dodgers (Baseball team)—History.] I. Title.
GV875.B7R67 1991
796.357'64'0974723—dc20
90–36691 CIP
AC

To Barbara and Anne

Buddy could hardly eat his breakfast. This was the day he and his pals were going to a Brooklyn Dodgers Knot Hole Game.

Kids who went to school in Brooklyn could become members of the Knot Hole Club, which was sponsored by the Dodgers. Belonging to the club meant members could go to a Dodgers baseball game free. Usually a whole school or a neighborhood of schools went to the same game. Today was Brooklyn Day and the schools were closed.

The pals met on Buddy's front stoop. Elliot the Announcer was not a great ball player, but he loved to announce ball games. He would sit on the curb, imaginary microphone in hand, announcing the play-by-play of any stickball game going on. Marty Hammer, called the Hammer, was a notorious New York Giants fan and a pretty good first baseman. Herby the Honker could make a wonderful loud noise like a car horn. It could be heard a block away. Nootie Lippman, whose real first name no one ever remembered, was famous for his unending appetite. He was the team catcher because he owned the catcher's equipment. Buddy was called the Handyman because he seemed to have so many hands playing shortstop.

They all (except the Hammer) loved the Dodgers, nicknamed the Bums, just as their fathers loved the Dodgers and probably their grandfathers, too! They knew the names of all the players, the positions they played, and their batting averages.

That year, 1946, was special, because World War II had ended and the players had returned from the army, navy, and marines. The gang was going to be able to see old favorites like Pee Wee Reese and Pete Reiser. And there was a rookie center fielder named Carl Furillo.

This was also an especially important game because the Dodgers were playing the New York Giants, their longtime rivals. The Giants were from Manhattan, across the river, and played at a stadium called the Polo Grounds.

The gang members were all prepared for the big day. They carried their mitts, and each one had a shoe box or paper bag full of lunch and snacks.

Tossing a baseball among them, the Handyman to the Hammer to the Honker and over Elliot's head to Nootie, they made their way to the subway, which in that part of Brooklyn was on an elevated track.

On the train they began arguing about who was a better manager, Mel Ott of the Giants or Brooklyn's Leo Durocher. They discussed their favorite players and why Carl Furillo was going to be the best Brooklyn center fielder ever. They started eating their sandwiches. Marty the Hammer traded a baloney sandwich for one of Nootie's salami sandwiches. While Elliot ate his baloney sandwich, he interviewed the Handyman about who would win the National League championship.

They got off the train at the Prospect Park station. The streets were full of people walking toward the stadium. As they got nearer, they were joined by more and more people. Soon they were part of a marching army of fans all going to Ebbets Field, home of the Brooklyn Dodgers.

The Knot Hole kids all sat in the upper left field stands. As they made their way to their seats, the guys said "Hey" to a lot of their friends and schoolmates. Everybody was eating lunch and watching the Dodgers warm up. The left field stands smelled like a delicatessen.

Buddy loved Ebbets Field. He looked out at the infield and diamond, the long green outfield, the big black scoreboard, and the billboards. A sign at the bottom of the scoreboard said HIT SIGN—WIN SUIT. It was put there by a famous Brooklyn shop owner.

Buddy couldn't understand how a kid who was born and raised in Flatbush, Brooklyn, like Marty the Hammer, could be a Giants fan.

Finally the game was about to start. The Dodgers ran out onto the field, and Elliot began to announce, "And now, ladies and gentlemen, the Dodgers take their positions on the playing field. Ed Stevens at first base; Eddie Stanky, second; the world's greatest shortstop, Pee Wee Reese; Cookie Lavagetto at third base; the right fielder, Dixie Walker; in center field, soon to be rookie of the year, Carl Furillo; and in left field, the one and only Pistol Pete Reiser. Catching is Bruce Edwards, and on the mound, their winningest pitcher, Kirby Higbe."

The Dodgers Sym-phony, a small band formed by musical Dodgers fans, played "Three Blind Mice" at almost every game, as the umpires strutted out.

The game began. There were a couple of scoreless innings, and then the Giants threatened, but Ed Stanky, playing second, snagged Johnny Mize's smash and tossed it to Pee Wee, who put out the Giants' Sid Gordon, at second base. Pee Wee threw to Stevens at first to catch Mize. An inning-ending double play and END OF THREAT!

Buddy cheered and smacked his Pee Wee Reese mitt. The Honker gave out a special blast, and Elliot happily announced the play.

Johnny Mize, the Giants' slugging first baseman, smacked a homer. The Giants went ahead—Marty Hammer was the only kid in the gang who was happy.

Close play at first base! Dixie Walker was called out. Leo Durocher, also known as Leo the Lip, came out to argue with the umpire. The Dodgers Sym-phony struck up its umpire theme. Herby's honk carried over the roar of the left field bleachers.

It was now bottom of the eighth. The guys had eaten all the sandwiches, cookies, and fruit their mothers had packed for them. With Nootie in the lead, they had begun buying hot dogs, peanuts, and sodas.

PEANUTS
10¢

The Dodgers were still behind by one run. It was two out. Carl
Furillo was on second, and Pete Reiser smashed a long drive into the
left field stands.

A home run! All the guys reached for the ball, all except Elliot, who was excitedly announcing his first real game-winning Pistol Pete home run.

The ball smashed into the stands and bounced around among the kids.

Finally, Marty the Hammer snagged it and held it up triumphantly.

Buddy couldn't believe it. Marty the Hammer, the Giants fan, grabbed a Pete Reiser home run ball.

There was no justice!

With a smirk, Marty proclaimed that he'd keep the ball as a souvenir of the enemy, like a war trophy.

Top of the ninth, and to protect their lead, Durocher sent in Hugh Casey, the relief pitcher known as the Fireman.

The rest is history. The Dodgers won.

Nootie gulped down his last soda, Elliot signed off the air, and Herby gave a victory honk.

Buddy and the Hammer led the group down the exit ramp. Everybody was in a great mood because the Bums had won. Even Marty the Hammer was happy because of his trophy, which he tossed in the air as he walked.

The boys joined the army of fans leaving Ebbets Field. They crowded into the street, lined with hot dog stands, soda vendors, candy stores, and souvenir sellers, and were pushed toward the subway station.

The train pulled in. It was filled with people coming home from work.
As the gang piled into the train, the passengers asked the kids who had
won the game. When Elliot told them Brooklyn had, they cheered.

Walking home from the train, Elliot broadcast a recap of the whole game and interviewed all the guys, who made believe they were Pee Wee, Pistol Pete, Leo, and Mel Ott. Everybody was having a great time, even Buddy. He watched the Hammer toss his Pete Reiser home run ball into the air and thought, Some trophy! He didn't even catch it. It rolled to his feet.

At dinner that night, Buddy was still too excited about the game to eat. Or maybe it was the sandwiches, cookies, fruit, hot dogs, and soda. He replayed the game's highlights for his father, and when he got to the Pete Reiser home run, he realized he'd rather have the Dodgers win than catch a dumb home run ball.